Elephant in a Rowboat

For Mum, with love, Angela

For my Mum, with thanks and love, Holly

First published in Great Britain in 2004 by

Gullane Children's Books

an imprint of Pinwheel Limited

Winchester House, 259-269 Old Marylebone Road,
London NW1 5XJ

1 3 5 7 9 10 8 6 4 2

Text © Angela McAllister 2004
Illustrations © Holly Swain 2004

The right of Angela McAllister and Holly Swain
to be identified as the author and illustrator of this work
has been asserted by them in accordance with the
Copyright, Designs and Patents Act, 1988.

A CIP record for this title is available from the British Library.

ISBN 1 86233 225 8

Printed and bound in Belgium

Elephant in a Rowboat

Angela McAllister   Holly Swain

GULLANE
CHILDREN'S BOOKS

Once there was a boy called Max who
came down to the edge of a lake.
He wanted to cross to the other side.
There wasn't a bridge.
There weren't any stepping stones.

But

in the middle
of the lake there
was an elephant
in a rowboat.

Max watched the rowboat.
It didn't move nearer.
It didn't move further away.
"Hey, Little Elephant," called
Max, "bring back the boat."

"I can't! I dropped the oars," wailed
the elephant. "And I've been here
a long time, and

I'm
hungry!"

Max took off his cap and pulled out a bag of doughnuts.
He skimmed a doughnut across the water, then
another and another.

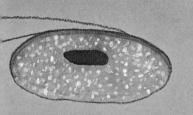 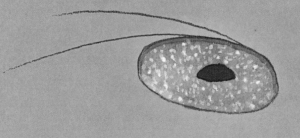 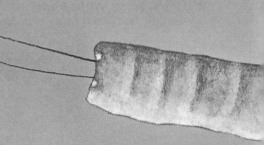

The elephant caught them with his trunk.
"Mmm, jammy ones, my favourite," he said.

Along danced a pink spangly ballerina.
She tripped to the edge of the lake
on her tippy toes.
"Oh, Little Elephant," she cried,
"will you row me across?"

The elephant
shook his head.
"I can't," he replied.
"I'm stuck!"

"Oh dear," sighed
the ballerina. "Then
I shall sing to you."

La la la la la

And as she sang
she practised pointing

la la la la la

on her pointy pointes.

Two thin men in fat men's trousers climbed out of a rattly car.

"He has to get across," said one.

"And I have to get across," said the other.

"So do I,"
said the elephant, "but I'm stuck!"
He swung his trunk glumly.

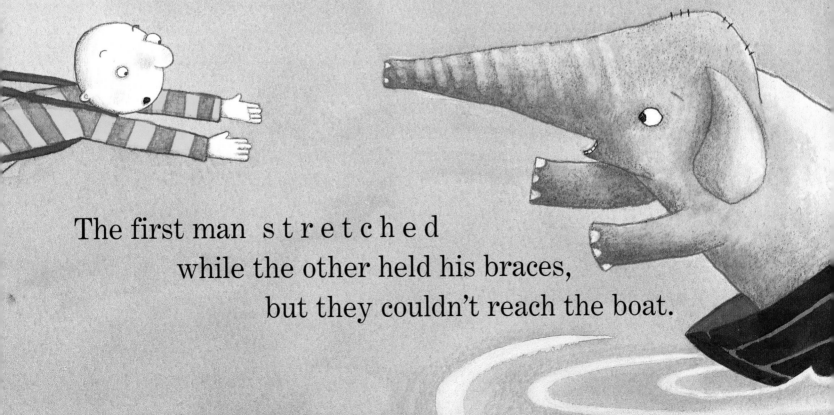

The two men dismantled their car
and built a jetty from the bank.

The first man s t r e t c h e d
while the other held his braces,
but they couldn't reach the boat.

"Boo hoo!" cried the two thin men.
"Time for a custard pie."

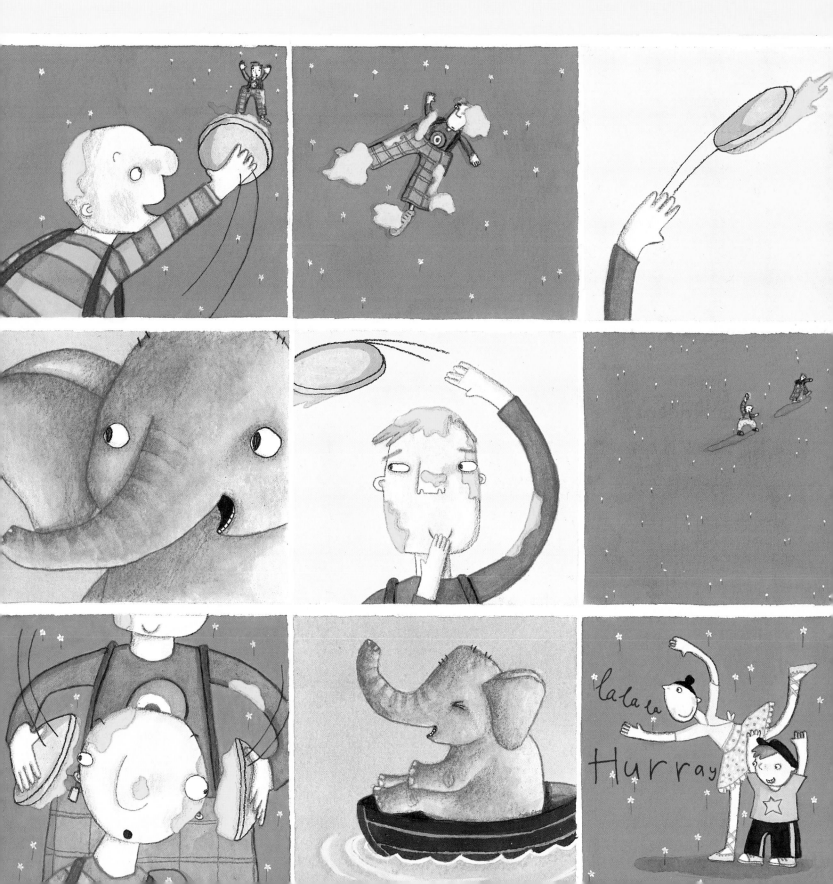

And soon they were slipping and sliding in a
puddle of custard to keep the elephant happy.

Suddenly a *thunderrrummmble* rolled across the lake.

"I'm still **hungry!**" said the elephant.

Max took more doughnuts out of his cap.
He frisbeed them across the water.

"Mmm,
sugary ones,
my favourite,"
said the elephant.

A man with a handlebar moustache marched down to the lake. "Ho, Little Elephant!" he bellowed. "Row along there." "I can't!" said the elephant. "I'm in a bit of trouble!"

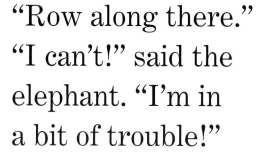

The moustache man lifted up a big rock and threw it into the water,

then another,

then another...

He jumped onto the rocks,
but he couldn't reach the boat.

"Well, it's a good spot for jogging on the spot," said the moustache man. And as he jogged, he

juggled

for the little elephant.

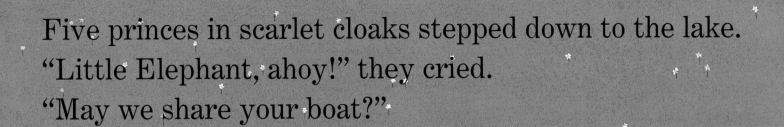

Five princes in scarlet cloaks stepped down to the lake.
"Little Elephant, ahoy!" they cried.
"May we share your boat?"

"The boat
can't move!"
said the elephant,
"and nor can I!"

The five princes took off
their cloaks and climbed
up into a tree that grew
over the water.

They held each other

by the ankles and swung far out,

but they could not

"We could play *What am I?*"
said the five princes.

But the elephant
guessed every time!

reach the boat.

Once more a *thunderrrumm* rolled across the lake.
"I'm still **hungry!**" said the elephan

Max took a bag of peanuts out of his cap.
He flung them across the water.

ble

The elephant caught them with his trunk.
"Mmm, fat salty ones, my favourite," he said.
But when he'd licked his sticky lips the little elephant frowned.
"I'm thirsty!" he cried.
"Have a drink," said Max.

Slowly the elephant in the rowboat stood up. He dipped his trunk into the water and took a sip. Then he began to suck.

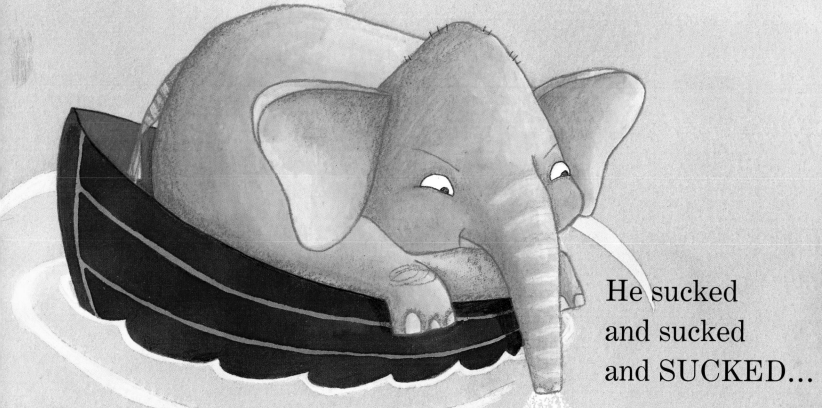

He sucked and sucked and SUCKED...

until he had sucked up every drop of water!
All that was left was a puddle for the fishes.

At that moment a man
in a very tall hat walked down
to where the lake had been –
and straight across
to the other side.

The elephant stepped out
of the rowboat and followed.

Everyone cheered!

Then Max and the
spangly ballerina, the
thin men in fat men's trousers,
the moustache man and the
five princes with scarlet cloaks
all followed to the other side.

When everyone was across,
the elephant lowered his trunk
and blew the water back again.

Then he picked up Max
and sat him on his back.

"Well done, Little Elephant!" said Max.

"**NOW!**" announced the man in the very tall hat, in a very loud voice, "**NOW**, LADIES AND GENTLEMEN, BOYS AND GIRLS, **NOW** IT IS TIME

FOR THE **CIRCUS!**"

And Max tossed his elephant keeper's cap high into the air. "Hurray!" he cheered, for so it was.